DEFENDERS
★ OF THE ★
UNIVERSE

D. V. Kelleher

Illustrated by Jane Clark Brown

Houghton Mifflin Company
Boston 1993

Text copyright © 1993 by Daria V. Kelleher
Illustrations copyright © 1993 by Jane Clark Brown

Library of Congress Cataloging-in-Publication Data

Kelleher, D. V. (Daria V.)
   Defenders of the universe / D.V. Kelleher ; illustrated by Jane
Clark Brown.
      p.   cm.
   Summary: A group of six kids band together in a "superhero" group
and eventually put their play skills to practical use.
   ISBN 0-395-60515-6
      [1. Heroes — Fiction.   2. Clubs — Fiction.   3. Criminals —
Fiction.]   I. Brown, Jane Clark, ill.   II. Title.
PZ7.K21825De   1993   92-1617
[Fic] — dc20   CIP
                             AC

Printed in the United States of America

VB   10 9 8 7 6 5 4 3 2 1

For Herb Rader

With thanks to my critics:
Melissa Trozzolillo, Elizabeth Forslund,
Rachel Forslund, Kristin AtLee, Erin AtLee,
Shannon Prime, Shannon Beck, and Richard Graber

Contents

★ 1 ★

The Defenders

I sure as heck didn't know what I was getting into when I joined the Defenders of the Universe.

I mean, they looked like the geeks of the whole school and I'm not a geek, no way. At least I wasn't at my last school. But then we had to move here. My parents told me, "You'll make new friends," like it's so easy to do. And guess what? One of these Defenders is only in kindergarten. Just tell me how many sixth-graders you know who hang out with babies. Anyway, it all started when I was sitting in the park, minding my own business, reading a comic book.

"Hi."

I turned my head and saw this little kid sitting next to me. He was kind of cute with his golden-colored hair and his big blue eyes. He was staring at me real intense.

"Are you lost or something?"

"No." He just smiled. "What's your name?"

I wanted to get back to my comic book, but there was something weird about this kid.

"Rachel," I told him. "What's yours?"

"Cranium."

"Cranium? What kind of name is that? Isn't that a skull or something?" Before he could answer, we were suddenly surrounded by this group of kids. I mean, they just beamed in from nowhere. "How did you do that?" I yelled at them. But I knew who they were. They were all from my new school. The short blond kid was Christopher and the black kid was Kyle. Carlotta was the Hispanic girl with the backpack and the other girl was Minh. I knew Minh was Vietnamese or something.

"Justin, you're not supposed to tell people your secret identity," Christopher said. "That's why we call it secret." I figured Justin was Christopher's little brother because Christopher sounded the way your parents do when they have to tell you the same thing a hundred times.

"Secret identity? So what are you guys, Super Heroes or something? And how come he" — I pointed my thumb at Justin — "has a name like Cranium?"

"He's the one with the psychic powers and we couldn't call him Braniac or Mentor. Those names are taken." Christopher folded his arms across his chest. "Anyway, can you come up with a better one?"

I read a lot of comic books and there are a bunch of heroes and villains with mental powers. All the good names *were* taken.

"Who are you?" I was starting to get interested — I couldn't help it. Christopher didn't ask what I meant, he knew.

"I'm the leader of the Defenders of the Universe. I'm Captain Hero." He pointed at Kyle. "This is U.N. for United Nations. He's the guardian of peace and wisdom. Packy" — he flung his arm out toward the girl with the backpack — "has anything we could possibly need on a mission, and Critter — "

The girl Minh pushed his arm away. "I'm Animal Princess, not Critter." She glared at him. "I have control over animals."

They all stood there real serious and I felt like laughing, but I wanted to know more about them. Why had they come looking for me and how did they know that my most secret wish in the world was to be a Super Hero?

"So do you guys have costumes?"

"Of course we do." Christopher acted like it was a stupid question.

"Well, like can I see them?"

"Not yet. We have to see what your 'power' is, figure out if we can use it."

"Hey, wait a minute. Are you the only one who does the talking? Maybe I don't want to defend the universe or wear leotards." Who did this jerk think he was, anyway? The little kid tugged at my sleeve.

"I found you with my powers. You hafta be one."

"What are you talking about, kid, you mean your mental powers?" I didn't want to be mean to Justin; he seemed like a nice little kid.

"We sent Cranium out to find a new member because Silver Skater moved away. You should've seen him. His costume was all silver and he could skate so fast." Packy, finally speaking up, must have liked this guy Silver Skater. So they sent Cranium out to find a new member. It couldn't have been too hard for him. I was sitting here reading a Super Hero comic book. I looked over at Cranium. Don't worry kid, I'll never tell. He grinned up at me as though he knew what I was thinking, but how could he hear my thoughts?

"So do you want to join or not?"

Did I?

I sure did, but I didn't want to look too anxious to Chris.

"Look, why don't we meet here tomorrow and I'll give you my decision?" It was something a Super Hero might have said, so I gave them my most serious look.

"Okay," said Captain Hero. "In the meantime, we have work to do."

They turned around and, without looking back, left the park.

The Avengers couldn't have done it better.

★ 2 ★

The Power Search

"First of all, how come you are the Defenders of the Universe? Why not just defend the Earth?" We were back at the park the next day and I was stalling for time.

"Do you think we are the only life in the universe?" Kyle asked in his solemn voice.

"Of course not." What did he think I was, a dummy?

Christopher said, "Well, what if a UFO landed here and asked for our help? What are we going to say, 'No, we only defend the Earth?' They'd never come back here again and they'd probably tell all the other aliens, 'Don't bother with Earth. Humans are jerks.'"

He had a point there.

"So are you going to let me see your costumes?"

"We're wearing them!" Packy grinned at me, delighted that I'd asked.

Wow, just like real Super Heroes, they must have their costumes on under their clothes, I realized.

"Do you want to be a Defender?" Chris asked finally.

My time ran out. "Look, you guys, I really do, but I can't think of a single power that I have." There, I had finally admitted it. I had stayed awake half the night trying to think of something I could do. I'd failed.

To my surprise, they didn't get up and leave.

"Cranium says you have something," Packy insisted.

I sighed. "Maybe he's wrong this time."

Chris stood up and brushed the grass off his pants. "I think we should show you our costumes and tell you our powers and maybe that will help you think of something."

"Would you? That would be great!"

"Come on."

We walked into the wooded area of the park and climbed a hill. Following a narrow dirt path, we came to a little clearing. The trees kept out any noise and the green coolness made a great place for secrets. I sat down on a rock and waited.

Suddenly I was all alone. "Hey, where are you guys?"

"Just stay where you are," Chris yelled from behind some trees. So I did.

There was a blur and Chris stood in front of me. He wore red, white, and blue, of course. His cape reached to the back of his knees and the emblem on his chest was a gold C. His red tights disappeared into black rubber rain boots.

"Rain boots?" I asked with raised eyebrows.

He grinned and held up one foot so I could see the bottom. "Good traction."

Carlotta was next. As Packy, she had on a pale blue leotard and tight set with a dark blue flared ice skating skirt that was short in the front and dipped in the back to a sharp point. She wore a dark blue backpack and dark blue sneakers. She bounced up and down smiling shyly until Chris motioned for her to stand next to him.

"Think of something that we might need on a mission," Chris challenged me.

"Uh, how about a flashlight?"

Packy pulled off her backpack and unzipped it. She set a flashlight on the ground.

"A disguise." A hat was set down next to the flashlight.

"String." String appeared.

"Emergency rations." A package of crackers was next.

"Okay, okay, what about money for a pay phone?" A little change purse came from another pocket.

"Wow, Packy! That's terrific!"

She repacked everything quickly and put
the backpack on again.

"Now we have U.N."

It wasn't Kyle who came out, though. It was Justin.

"I want to be next, Chris. Tell her my powers."

Chris scowled for a minute. "All right. But go back and do it right."

Justin ran back behind the trees. When he came back out he was squinting his eyes and holding his hands to his forehead.

"Justin, you look like you have a headache. Can't you do any better than that?"

With a flash of temper Justin yelled, "You said to hold my hands up!"

"Wait a minute!" I said. "Justin, how about this?" I showed him my idea of bending his hands at the wrists and just touching his temples at both sides. He tried it himself and looked pretty good.

"Cranium, who can sense other people's thoughts and detect the presence of evil aliens." Cranium wore all black. It made the silver circle on his chest really stand out. I stooped down and touched the circle. It was made of silver reflecting tape and had a pattern of tiny diamonds all over it. Cranium proudly traced the circle with one finger.

Cranium sat next to me and Captain Hero went on.

"Now we have U.N., the keeper of peace and knowledge." Kyle stepped into the clearing and bowed. He was a blaze of color. His leotard was blue with scarlet sleeves, the tights had one emerald green leg and one golden yellow leg, and his trunks were black. His emblem was gold crossed wheat.

"As you can see, U.N. wears the same colors as the Olympic symbol — "

"How come?" I interrupted.

"Because one of these colors is in every country's flag in the world," Kyle answered with his arms straight out at his sides.

"What's your power — "

"If you'll just let me finish!" yelled Captain Hero.

"Okay! Go on!" I shouted back.

"U.N. knows all about the countries of the

world, and his duty is to keep peace between nations — "

"But — "

" — Or people!" Captain Hero glared at me.

"I bet he has his work cut out for him here," I mumbled. U.N. smiled and winked at me.

"What did you say?" Captain Hero asked in an ominous voice.

"I said who made these fantastic costumes?"

Packy said, "He did," and pointed at U.N. "He's going to be a famous designer when he grows up."

I turned to Kyle with new respect.

"I only sewed the emblems and designed the costumes," he began modestly. "We bought the leotards and tights."

"So what, they're still good — "

We heard a cough from behind the tree and I remembered Minh.

"And of course — Animal Princess, controller of animals and friend to all who wear fur or feathers!"

Minh, who was the prettiest girl I had ever

seen, walked gracefully out from behind the tree and I saw what must have been Kyle's masterpiece. Her leotard and tights were a light tan and her short skirt was made of material with leopard spots. The hem was cut kind of ragged to make it look like a real leopard skin, and a black felt panther head with white sequin teeth was sewed on her chest.

"Kyle, would you do a costume for me?"

"Sure." He gave me a sunny smile.

"We don't know who you are going to be yet," Captain Hero reminded me.

Packy leaned forward. "What can you do?" she asked earnestly.

"I can't really do anything."

"Everybody can do something," the Captain insisted.

"Are you strong?" Cranium asked me.

I stopped and thought about it. I *had* helped my mother carry some pretty heavy packing boxes when we moved.

"Well, I can lift heavy things," I answered thoughtfully.

"We don't have a strong person," Packy began, then shot the Captain a look, "except Captain Hero," she finished diplomatically.

"The Captain is supposed to be our leader. He can't run around and do strength stuff too," U.N. stated firmly. They all waited for the Captain to say something. He seemed to struggle for a minute, then said, "You guys are right. I can't do everything." He looked at me then.

"What do you want your name to be?"

"I know, I know!" Packy jumped up and down, excited. "What about Power Force?"

"Those words mean the same thing," Minh said scornfully.

"It just means she has to be really strong." Packy waited for my answer.

I repeated the name a couple of times. I had to admit it had a good sound to it.

"I like it, Packy," I told her and she beamed at me.

"What will her colors be?" the Captain asked U.N.

U.N. absently rubbed his chin with one finger. "Power," he mumbled thoughtfully.

"Can you get your parents to buy you a leotard and tights? They're not cheap. It took us months to earn the money," Captain Hero asked me.

"I think so." I knew I would have no trouble there. My father and mother were always after me to make new friends, and if it meant having tights they wouldn't care.

"Purple," U.N. finally said.

We looked at him blankly.

"Purple is the color of power," he explained. "That's why kings wore it. Nobody else was allowed to." He stared at me intently, but I knew he wasn't seeing me. I knew what he needed, so I handed him the sketchbook I always had with me. He flipped it open and got to work.

"You better tell her the secret stuff," Minh told the Captain. I studied her, curious about why she didn't talk more. How the heck had she gotten in with this rowdy group?

"Right." The Captain was all business again. He held out his hand to Packy. She pulled some papers out of her backpack.

"You have to memorize this stuff and then destroy these papers."

I studied the paper on top, which was a map of some kind.

"This is our city." The Captain leaned forward to point it out. "We divided it into parts and named each part after a country. That's so you can tell one of us the location of something and no one else will know what you're talking about. We did it like the real world so that the downtown area is called America and the part north is Canada and south is Mexico. It's easier to remember that way."

I groaned inside. It wasn't easy for me. I didn't know doodly-squat about geography. Well, I was just going to have to learn.

"Since the America part is big, we use the states to narrow down an area," the Captain went on. "So if you mean City Hall, you say 'Maine' and if you mean the library you say

'Nevada.'" He searched my face to see if I understood. I understood that I was going to be doing more homework than I usually did for school. Where was Maine and where was Nevada?

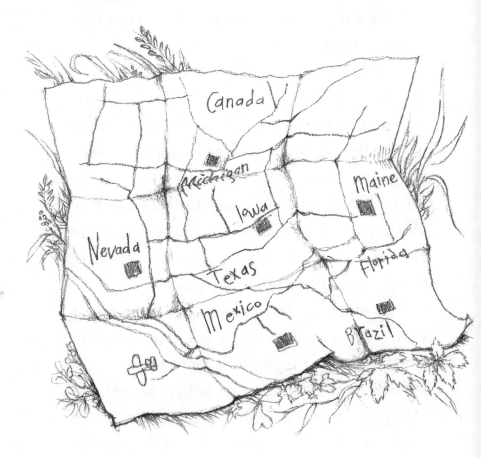

"I get it. Where is school?"

"Down here in Brazil."

I was thinking, Wasn't Brazil in Africa, when Cranium suddenly said to U.N., "Silver."

"Just what I was thinking." U.N. nodded absently.

The Captain glanced down at his brother and saw the tiredness. "We have to go now." He stood up and started to detach his cape. "Whenever we have a meeting, you'll get a piece of paper marked with a star. It's our symbol."

I collected my sketchbook from U.N. and they all put their clothes back on over their costumes. Wow, soon I would have a costume too. I felt that I should say something, so I said, "Hey, it's going to be great working with you guys."

"You're not in yet," the Captain reminded me, pulling a sweatshirt over his head.

I started to come back with something but clamped my mouth shut. How come he always had to have the last word? I'd worry about that later, for now I was sure glad that I had found this group.

I forgot that they were the ones who found me.

★ 3 ★

The First Case

"You want me to go shopping with Justin and Kyle?" I asked Christopher.

"Yeah. What's wrong with that?"

He knew very well what was wrong with it. Me shopping with two boys. What the heck did boys know about clothes?

"Anyway, Kyle is making your costume. You can't get anything without his approval."

"Now just a minute here — " I started hotly.

Packy tugged at my sleeve.

"What!" I unfairly turned my anger on her.

"You have to go with them because Minh can't go today and I have patrol duty. Chris is

23

our leader." She added that at the end.

Didn't I just know that. And they all followed his orders like a bunch of sheep.

Cranium giggled and said, "Sheeps."

Sometimes that kid made me nervous. He really did seem to pick up thoughts. And what about Packy? People getting mad and yelling didn't seem to bother her. Was I wrong this time?

"Okay. Come on, let's go." I turned my back on Chris and headed for my bike. Behind me, I heard him get on his own bike and cut through the trees to the back exit from the park.

Packy was the only one in uniform today because she had patrol duty. She zipped up her jacket to cover her insignia and walked her bike behind us, studying Chris's map for this week's patrol. I cheered up a little bit as I thought about how I would do patrols when it was my turn. The Defenders did one patrol a week, and it was always in a different area. We were supposed to keep an eye on things and make sure nothing was happening like evil aliens moving in or super villains causing trouble. Once, on his patrol, Kyle had seen some boys climbing in the window of a dark house. He hid in the bushes and watched until he realized that the boys lived there and had locked themselves out accidently. Chris said it didn't matter if it wasn't a real emergency, Kyle was a good patroller. Well, wait until they saw me.

We had just reached the street when it happened. A big blue car squealed around the corner and came roaring down the street toward us. Luckily, we were still on the sidewalk.

Justin screamed.

I jerked my head around and saw the lady in the crosswalk. I screamed too when the car hit her. I couldn't believe what had just happened, and I stood there frozen as the man in the car turned to look at me and then drove off. It was like time had slowed down. I only saw him for a second, but I remembered every part of his face. At the same time, I saw Packy drop her bike and run back toward the park while Kyle cautiously stepped into the street and then ran to the lady. He jerked his arms out of his jacket and gently placed it over her. I still couldn't move and I felt numb all over, but I finally heard someone crying and I forced myself to turn my head. Justin stood on the curb, and his crying got wilder as he clutched the side of his face. That finally broke the spell. I ran over and tried to put my arms around him.

"Justin, it's going to be okay."

"She's hurt!" He drew in a long, sobbing breath.

"Justin, listen!" We both heard the sirens getting closer. Justin stopped to listen and just hiccuped a few times instead of making that awful wailing noise. "Justin! We have to do something," but I didn't know what. Packy ran toward us and stopped, out of breath.

"I told them that we needed police *and* an ambulance."

"You called the police?"

She nodded and then took Justin's hand.

I just stood there. I had seen the accident too, but I hadn't done anything. Packy had gone for a phone and Kyle had tried to help the lady. I felt my face go red with shame. I wanted to be a Defender and I hadn't done a single thing. I didn't want to go shopping. I wanted to go home and get under the bed because I didn't deserve to be a Defender. Just then I felt a small hand in mine and I looked down into Justin's tearstained little face.

"You are a Defender. You can do something too."

Before I had a chance to ask what he meant, an ambulance and a bunch of police cars pulled up. The Defenders were just a bunch of kids in the way. We stepped back onto the curb as another car stopped and a man got out. I guess it was an unmarked police car because you could tell this man was in charge. He was tall and kind of thin, but you could tell that he was a strong kind of thin. Even through his glasses, his eyes were real intense. One of the officers, a blond lady, walked over to him with a clipboard.

"Okay, all you kids head on home." Another officer herded us back.

"But we're witnesses!" Packy told him.

"That's right, go on home."

We looked at each other.

"Maybe we should talk to the guy in charge," Packy whispered. The guy in charge looked pretty busy, though, so we turned toward our bikes. I forgot that I was still holding Justin's hand until he refused to budge.

"Justin, they don't want to hear from a bunch of kids, so come on."

"You saw him."

I sighed and said, "And I suppose you won't come with us until I tell him, right?"

He nodded.

"All right, all right."

I started to walk over, but with each step I got more nervous. When I was in front of the officer, he turned that glow-in-the-dark look at me.

"Excuse me, sir, but I saw the guy who did it." I waited for him to tell me to get lost.

"It was a man driving the car?"

"Yes, sir." Wow, didn't they even know *that*?

"Sergeant! We have a witness over here!" The blond lady came back, and I could tell that she didn't want a kid for a witness.

"Now what exactly did you see? Take your time," the man said.

I told them.

"You saw the man's face clearly? Would you be able to recognize him again?"

"Oh yes, sir." Then I had an idea. "Would you like me to draw him for you?" I started to get out my sketchpad.

He was surprised but told me to go ahead. I sat down on the curb and drew the face that was so clear in my mind.

The man, who was called Lieutenant by the other officers, studied the picture.

"This is very good, very clear. Write your name and phone number in the corner here."

The Sergeant peeked over my shoulder and said, "You know, this guy looks familiar for some reason."

"Make copies of this and be sure everyone in the station gets a copy. Maybe this guy has been stopped for reckless driving or something. Also, check all the bulletins."

The Lieutenant turned his attention to me.

"Good job, kid. What's your name?"

"Rachel Cotter."

"Well, I'm Lieutenant Stefano. I'll probably be in touch."

The Defenders were waiting for me at the curb.

"Wow!" Packy breathed. "You'll probably be the main reason that they crack the case!"

"Maybe you have the wrong power," U.N. added.

"What?"

He grinned. "Maybe you shouldn't be Power Force after all."

"Oh yeah, sure. So who am I going to be, Drawer, the Defender who can draw? That sounds pretty stupid. There I am, running around with a sketchpad strapped to my waist, yelling, 'Stop! Before I draw you!' Right, you guys."

Justin giggled, but U.N. studied me thoughtfully.

"I see you in a light violet leotard with silver trim. We could call you . . ."

"The Sketcher!" Packy shouted triumphantly.

"You could have a silver pencil and notebook," U.N. went on. "We would need you to sketch crime scenes and keep drawings of suspects."

"What kind of emblem would I have?" I was interested in spite of myself.

"A silver pencil crossed with a bolt of lightning."

"Kyle, could you do that?"

"Uh-huh. I think we better get going, I need to get started right away."

Suddenly I realized that I *wanted* to be

Sketcher because it was something I could do. I really did have a power!

"Well, let's get going then! See you later, Packy, and watch for the suspect!"

"Got it!" She ran to her bike and hopped on.

"Hmmmmm."

"What is it, Kyle?"

"Maybe we shouldn't be planning your costume without the Captain's okay. And we don't know what Minh thinks, either."

"Who cares what they think? It's my power!"

"The Captain is in charge," Kyle reminded me firmly.

I stopped myself before I said something rude about the Captain, who was Justin's brother.

"Look, you guys, I'll take responsibility for it. If the Captain doesn't like it, I'll use the costume for exercising in or something."

They didn't have a problem with that, so

we headed for the stores downtown. Actually, I wanted the costume finished before the Captain found out, because I *was* going to be the Sketcher whether he liked it or not. We would just see what Mr. Super Hero Leader thought of that.

★ 4 ★

The Sketcher

Captain Hero was livid.

"You can't go around doing things without everybody's approval!" he shouted into my face. The others just stood around silently. I wore my new costume and it was really something. The leotard was a lovely light violet color and since we had been unable to find matching tights, I wore a pair that were a shimmery silver. The short skirt was silver too and made of a material that looked like metal but was light like tissue. Kyle had made the emblem out of that liquid embroidery stuff and stuck it on with Velcro, which I told him

was a stroke of genius. He had been embarrassed.

Chris was finished yelling and just stood
there glaring at me.

"Look, I'm sorry. It was my idea to go ahead
with it and I just didn't think you'd make a
big deal out of it."

That major lie made him even madder.

"You made a decision that you weren't supposed to make! This is a group, we make decisions together. You're used to having your
own way!"

I started to make a smart answer but
stopped. I really did want to be a Defender
and lying made me uncomfortable. I would
just have to try to get along with Chris.

He was waiting for me to answer.

I sighed and threw up my hands. "What do
you want me to say? I should've waited. Okay,
I'm sorry."

He eyed me suspiciously.

"Come on, Chris! You're right! Can we go

on now? Do I get to keep this costume or not?"
I took my hands off my hips and said in a
quieter voice, "Am I the Sketcher?" Please,
please, please, I thought.

He drew a deep breath and glanced around
at the others.

"What do you guys think?"

"Oh, let her keep it!" said Packy. "She really did help the police."

Chris's mouth thinned out, and I suddenly
understood the real reason for his anger. All
the Defenders but he and Minh were working
with the police on an important case.

Minh said, "It would cost money to make
another costume."

"I like it," Justin piped up.

Kyle said he wouldn't vote because he had
made the costume.

Captain Hero studied me, and I couldn't resist giving him a goofy smile. For once I did
the right thing. He rolled his eyes and said
resignedly, "Okay, you're the Sketcher. Let's

have the ceremony tomorrow."

They all cheered and I asked, "What ceremony?" but they just grinned at me.

I stood in a clearing in my regular afterschool clothes and waited.

They marched from behind the trees in single file and lined up in a half circle around me. They wore full costume with an added touch that I had never seen — masks. The Captain's was fiery red; Justin's, coal black; Kyle's, yellow; Minh's, chocolate; and Packy's, royal blue. Minh's and Packy's were decorated with matching sequins.

"Wow! You guys look terrific!"

They stayed silent, though Justin wiggled and giggled a little.

"Rachel stand forward!" Captain Hero commanded.

I took a step toward them and held myself straight, chin up.

"Do you agree to abide by the rules of the

Defenders of the Universe?" Chris eyed me sternly.

"I do."

"Do you agree to fight evil wherever it is and help those in trouble?"

"Yes."

"Do you agree to wear a costume and be known as the Sketcher?"

"I do."

"Packrat?"

Packy stepped toward me and held out my folded uniform. I took it.

"Cranium?"

Cranium took two steps and handed me a silver-wrapped package.

"Open it," the Captain said.

I tore open the paper to find a silver notebook with gold stars and my name printed neatly. "Thank you, Packy," I said, knowing she must have done the decorating. "It's pretty." Packy blushed.

"U.N.?"

U.N. stepped forward and handed me another package. This one had a little drawstring bag made out of my extra skirt material. It was just the right size to hold my notebook. Clipped to the outside was a silver pencil.

"Animal Princess?"

Minh had my mask. It was dark purple with silver sequins. My arms were loaded up when the Captain stepped forward. He put a silver cardboard star on top of the pile.

"This is the silver star, symbol of the Defenders. Use it wisely and in secret."

Finally they stood in a circle, and everybody put one hand out and we made a stack.

"We swear to defend the universe!"

This was great. I was so happy that I wanted to hug them all.

"Welcome." The Captain held his hand out. As I shook it, I decided that he wasn't so bad.

"Let's have the party!"

We had cupcakes baked by Chris and Justin, Kool-Aid made by Packy, and chips contributed by Kyle. Minh had the napkins and paper cups.

"Look, you guys," I told them seriously. "Thanks for letting me be in this club. I'll really do my best to be a good Defender."

And I really meant it.

★ 5 ★

The Evil Brain

I don't remember how we got started on the Evil Brain. Probably we got the idea from a comic book or movie. It was just a private joke.

"Justin, how could you forget to give me Kyle's message? It was important." Chris faced his brother, exasperated.

Justin bowed his head and didn't say anything, so I said, "He must've been taken over by the Evil Brain."

Justin giggled at me and slid a sideways look at Chris.

"Yeah, I know, except the Evil Brain has been taking him over a lot lately."

"Well, we'll have to find the Brain and send

43

it back to space or something."

"Sure, you do that. Keep an eye out for it on your patrol."

We all laughed.

I was bundled up good for my patrol, including muffler, hat, and gloves. I looked more like an Arctic explorer than a Super Hero, but *I* knew that underneath all of it was my uniform. Yeah, that was my secret.

I was steering around a piece of ice in the road when I saw him. I was so surprised that I hit the ice and my bike slid out from under me.

"Are you okay?" a lady with a shopping bag asked me.

I was saying some nasty words under my breath, but I was very glad that I had my heavy winter pants on over my tights. They would have been totaled.

"Uh yes, thank you. I'm wearing a lot of padding."

The kind face smiled and she said, "Aren't we all?"

I got back on my bike.

"I'm telling you guys, I saw the Evil Brain and he was just walking down the street!"

"What did he look like?" the Captain asked.

"He looked evil, what do you think?"

"How did he look evil?" The Captain was speaking slowly, trying to be patient.

"Here, I drew a quick sketch of him." I pulled my silver bag open and handed them the tablet.

"He *does* look like an Evil Brain," Minh volunteered.

I studied the picture myself. The man had silver-gray hair and a thin nose, but what really grabbed you were his eyebrows. They were sharp and pointed in the middle. His eyes appeared cold and watchful.

"He kind of looks like Magneto," Packy decided.

Magneto was a bad guy in our favorite comic, "The New Mutants."

"No, he looks eviler than Magneto."

"There's no such word as 'eviler,'" the Captain told his brother scornfully. Justin just shrugged and smiled at me.

"So what are we going to do about it?"

"We better keep an eye on him," the Captain said firmly. "From now on, all patrols will be downtown until we figure out what to do."

So we followed the Evil Brain.

We knew where he worked and where he shopped. We knew where he parked his car

during the day. We kept a diary on how he spent his weekends.

"This weekend," I read from my notebook, "he went to the mall on Saturday for about an hour, then he went home."

"Well, he doesn't do very much evil stuff," Justin pointed out.

Packy, who had been quiet, finally said, "I don't think it's very nice to follow people around."

"Why not?" I asked.

"I don't know. It's nosy."

"Maybe he's just acting normal to throw us

off while he plans something real big." The
Captain was always looking ahead.

That made sense.

"Hey, I just remembered. Justin, show everybody what you found at the card store." I
gently pushed him up front.

He pulled out a package of stickers and
proudly handed them to his brother. They
were glittery stars.

"This is great! Good job, Justin. I'll just
keep them in my pocket."

"Uh . . ." I pointedly looked down at Justin's bent head. "He found them, and he wants
everybody to have some."

I saw the familiar set of Chris's face as he
started to get angry.

"Where would you keep yours, Justin?"
Kyle hurriedly cut in.

Justin considered this. "In my lunchbox."

"You can't keep them in there, they'll get all
sticky. Here." Chris pulled a beat-up folder
out of his stack of books. "You can have this.

It has pockets and everything."

Justin smiled at his brother and I felt a sharp stab of jealousy. Justin always made me wish that he was my little brother. As usual, he picked up my thoughts, because he ripped open the package and handed me a sheet of stars, smiling at me before he handed out the rest.

"I want Rachel to keep some in her silver bag in case something happens to me."

"Nothing's going to happen to you, Justin. Come on, we better get home."

"Isn't that the Evil Brain over there?" I pointed to a man walking in our direction.

"Yes, but why is he walking down this way?" Packy asked, puzzled. "The only thing down here is the ferry."

I grabbed her arm, our shopping errand forgotten.

"That's it, Packy! He must be going to the airport! He's probably a smuggler or something. We have to follow him."

"No." Packy's eyebrows made a straight line across her face.

"What do you mean, no? We have to see what he's up to."

"He's not up to anything. I don't like this game anymore. There is no Evil Brain. This is a mean game."

"Packy, pleeeease! I don't have time to go get one of the others. Look," I said frantically, "I promise you that if he doesn't do anything suspicious, I'll quit the game myself."

"Really?" She still frowned.

"Really! Come on, we'll miss the ferry!"

"Okay," she said reluctantly. "Do we have enough money?"

We fished around in all our pockets quickly and found enough.

"Let's go!"

There weren't too many places to hide, so we just tried to look normal. Luckily, the Evil Brain seemed to have something on his mind. He never even looked at us.

"Probably trying to figure out where to hide the goods," I muttered darkly to Packy, who was silent.

When we got off the ferry, we dropped back a little but kept him in our sight. Inside the airport, we stood next to a pile of somebody's luggage and waited. I was hoping we wouldn't be here too long because my parents would kill me if they found out, and with my luck somebody who knew my parents was here getting on a plane. I shrunk back into some shadows. We heard the announcement of the flight arrival, and passengers started coming through the double doors.

"Daddy! Daddy!" I watched in amazement as a tiny little girl ran right to the Evil Brain. He scooped her up and hugged her, looking very happy and not evil at all.

I didn't say a word to Packy as we caught the first ferry back.

"I make a motion to stop following the Evil Brain," Packy announced at the next meeting.

"He's not evil, just a guy."

It was then that I understood something about Packy. She didn't like to look for the bad in people, even if it was just a game.

"Maybe he's just acting — "

I shook my head and held up my hand to Chris.

"She's right, Chris. The guy's some little kid's dad, for heaven's sake. He just acted suspicious because he missed her."

"I second the motion." U.N. raised his hand. "It was kind of a mean game, Chris. Super Heroes are supposed to set examples."

"Okay, okay. Everybody in favor of forgetting the Evil Brain say 'aye.'"

"Aye!" we all yelled.

And that was it — for a while, anyway.

★ 6 ★

Mutant Tarantula from Outer Space

"I wonder what those kids are doing over there?"

Minh looked up from the sidewalk and studied the group huddled around the curb. One of them shrieked and jumped back while the others laughed. Minh's face set in angry lines and she marched over to them, shoving one of the kids out of the way.

What the heck had gotten into her?

As I ran over, Minh scooped something up and started to walk away. The angry shouts of the kids followed her, but when she turned around to face them they suddenly got quiet. I understood when I saw her face.

"Wow, Minh, what's the matter? You look like you're going to rip somebody's head off."

"I will not stand around and watch anybody hurt an animal," she ground out between clenched teeth.

"They had an animal? What, a kitten or something? What did you do with it?" I looked around the street, but except for a brown dog sniffing a garbage can, there were no animals in sight.

"I took it from them." She opened her hands and I almost wet my pants.

"Aaaaaahhhhh! Are you crazy! Drop that thing!"

She just held that humongous brown and black hairy spider and glared at me.

"Minh, drop it! It will bite you and you'll die or something!"

She made a disgusted noise. "It's just a spider. I didn't think you were such a mush. You always talk brave."

Somehow her scorn was worse than anybody else's.

I stretched my neck to see the spider without moving any closer to her.

"See, he isn't biting me. Tarantulas are very friendly. Anyway, they sell them in pet stores, so how could they be dangerous?"

"Well, maybe they defang them or something." I thought of something else. "What is

he doing up here? We don't have any tarantulas in this state. They live in the desert or something."

"Then he must've been somebody's pet. They just got tired of him and dumped him to survive on his own." She glared around us as though we were going to find someone lurking in the bushes with an empty tarantula cage, or whatever they lived in.

"What are you going to do with him? Wait a second, how the heck do we even know it's a him?"

"It's a him," she said firmly.

"Okay, whatever. I guess *you* would know. Are you going to keep him?"

"Yes, he could be our mascot."

"A spider?" I said, incredulous.

"Not just a spider." She looked quite pleased with herself. "A Mutant Tarantula from Outer Space."

I started to giggle. "You know, that's not a bad idea. We should have a strange mascot. What shall we call him?"

"We better wait until we're all together," she said reproachfully.

"Yeah, you're right. I'll never get the hang of this group decision stuff."

"The Defenders of the Universe will now come to order. First order of business is the naming of our mascot, the Mutant Tarantula from Outer Space. Animal Princess thinks that we should draw lots for the privilege." Captain Hero addressed us at our usual place in the clearing.

I tore up some of my paper and put an X on one piece. Packy and I folded the pieces and dumped them in a paper bag. Oh sure, Packy even had a paper bag in her backpack.

"Everybody draw a paper."

"Who got it?" I looked around.

"I got it!" Justin jumped up and down, excited. "I get to name him!"

I groaned to myself. I had a whole bunch of names all ready. Justin couldn't possibly have any as good as mine.

Cranium threw back his shoulders. "I, Cranium, name the spider" — he paused to make sure we were all paying attention — "Captain Kirk!"

"Captain — ?"

"Oh man — "

Cranium's eyes drooped sadly.

"I think it's a great name and I second the motion," I yelled.

Captain Hero watched me, surprised, then his eyes caught Cranium's face too. "I third the motion!" he said quickly.

"It's a good name, Cranium," Packy put in.

"Would you like to hold him?" Minh asked, offering the spider to Cranium.

He appeared unsure for a second. "Yes!" He beamed at her.

I couldn't believe it. This little kid was going to hold that giant bug. Cranium was very gentle and the tarantula perched on his shoulder. "He likes me," he giggled, delighted.

I shuddered, but I felt Minh's eyes on me, so I clamped my teeth closed and reached one finger to pet the spider. He didn't jump or bite me so I rubbed him a little. He was kind of soft and I think he liked it.

"Hey, this isn't so bad," I announced.

Not to be outdone, Captain Hero gave him a tentative pat, then so did U.N. and Packrat. We grinned at one another.

So we had a spider named Captain Kirk, after Justin's favorite TV show. It could've been worse. He could have wanted to name it Enterprise.

★ 7 ★

Secret Signs

"Where's Captain Kirk?" I asked, searching the clearing. I wanted that spider where I could see it. Justin giggled, and I looked a little more closely at what I had thought was just a new hair style.

"Justin, that bug is sitting in your hair."

"He's a spider with eight legs, bugs have six legs," Packy informed me, sounding suspiciously like my teacher.

"Whatever. What's he doing there, anyway?"

Minh, who kept a watchful eye on Captain Kirk no matter who had him, answered, "He likes Justin and he likes to sit where he can see what's going on."

"Oh, that's fine," I said a little sarcastically. "But he doesn't, ah, leave anything in your hair, does he, Justin?"

"No spider poop." Justin laughed, quite tickled with himself.

Chris leaned over and studied his brother's hair, frowning, then straightened up.

"Let's come to order. U.N. has something he'd like to put before us."

U.N. cleared his throat. "As you know, I was put in charge of coming up with the Danger Signs, and I think I have a workable plan."

I rolled my eyes at Minh and Packy. Man, these guys got carried away sometimes.

U.N.'s plan was a good one, though. He called them the Danger Rocks. In front of every Defender's house would be a place where three rocks could be stacked one on top of the other. When Defenders went home at night, they were supposed to check to make sure that no one was in trouble in their family or that no evildoer had discovered their secret identity. If everything was okay, they were supposed to unstack the rocks. In the morning, before leaving for school, the rocks would be restacked.

Whoever had patrol duty would check all the houses before going off duty. Three rocks still stacked would be a sign of trouble.

"Yeah, but U.N., what if we just forget to move the rocks?" I wanted to know.

"You must try to remember," Captain Hero said sternly. "The Defender on patrol can always sneak up to a window in the house and peek in to see if everything looks normal if you forget to unstack your rocks." He made it sound as if I was the one who would forget all the time.

"I like it." Packy nodded.

"Okay, sounds good to me," I added.

Captain Hero waited for everyone's approval, then he said, "That's it for today. See you guys later." He stood up and brushed off the seat of his pants, then he and Kyle started talking about a video game. I turned to go and felt Justin tugging at my sleeve.

"What's up, Justin?"

"Rachel, I want to talk to you."

He looked so serious that I didn't even smile at the tarantula still crouched in his hair.

"Sure, go ahead."

He tugged me over to a log and I sat down.

"Rachel, what would you do if you were a mutant?"

"I don't know. What kind of mutant?"

"A mutant like me."

Whoa.

"Justin, being Defenders is just a game we play. We're not really mutants."

"Yes, I am," he insisted stubbornly. "I can read people's minds with my powers."

"Well, so what?" I said, suddenly switching directions. If I couldn't get him away from the mutant idea, I could try something else. But what?

He stared at me, wanting me to understand.

"I'm different from other people. What if they don't like it?"

"Justin, have you talked about this to Chris or anybody else?"

"Nobody would understand," he said sadly.

I was silent for a few minutes, thinking. I
didn't want to say the wrong thing. This was
very serious.

"Listen, Justin. I'm going home and I'll
think about this and I'll let you know what I
think tomorrow, okay?" That would give me
some time.

"Okay." He looked so relieved that it worried me. I watched him walk in his usual
jaunty way down the path and realized that I
hadn't seen that walk in a while. How long
had he been worrying about being a mutant?

Had the game gone too far for Justin?

"Hey, wait up for me!" I ran after him.

★ 8 ★
Cranium

"Dad, are you busy?"

It was a stupid question. My parents were always busy, but they tried to "be there for me" when they could.

My dad glanced at me, then turned his computer off.

"What is it, Babe?"

I knew the Defenders was secret, but after thinking about Justin all through dinner, I was worried. So I told my dad about the group, then I told him about Justin.

My dad didn't laugh, though he did grin a little bit. He held up his hand. "I'm not making fun of your group, Babe. I wish I had had a club like that when I was your age. It's very imaginative. Just don't get into anything over your head."

If you're wondering whether I told him about the Evil Brain, the answer is no. What am I, stupid?

"I think you can help Justin. First, try to get him away from this idea that he's a mutant." He saw my expression. "Won't work, huh?"

"I don't think so, Dad."

"Well, in that case, try to convince him that it's a gift and that humanity may need it in the future and that he should not let it control him. He must be in charge."

I nodded slowly.

"Will he understand that?"

"I think so." If I could say it to him right.

"As to being different, well, everybody worries about that at some time or another. Let me tell you a secret. When you get older, you will go out of your way to be different.

People hate being like everybody else. They want to stand out."

I would just have to take his word on that for now.

"Dad, do you think Justin needs, like counseling or something?"

"I don't know, Rachel. Maybe you could bring him by for a talk. I understand that his parents are divorced and he lives with his mother."

"You mean you could have a man-to-man talk?" I smiled.

He laughed. "Why not? Would he be upset that you told me about your group?"

"I don't know. But Dad, there's something else too. Lately Justin's been telling us that some danger is coming close to him. He says he picks it up with his powers. What the heck am I going to do about that?"

My dad sighed.

"Didn't you tell me that you met the Lieutenant from the police station?"

"Yes."

"Then why don't you ask the Lieutenant if he'll let you have a tour of the station. Maybe that will reassure Justin that the police are around for his protection. And it might be interesting for all of you to see how a police station works."

"Wow, Dad! That's a great idea! I'll bring it up with the Defenders tomorrow. Thanks!"

He grinned. "You know I'm here to help. Unless I'm baking chocolate chip cookies."

I laughed. My dad made some killer chocolate chip cookies. I threw my arms around his neck.

"That's it? You mean I solved all your problems in ten minutes?"

"You almost always do, Dad. That's why we keep you around."

He snorted and turned back to the computer screen. "You're begining to sound like your mother."

I went back to my room to get my school stuff ready. I couldn't wait for the next day.

★ 9 ★

The Tour

I brought my idea up the next day, and to my surprise Chris got enthusiastic about it. Sometimes I could really like him.

"You can call the Lieutenant and ask him when we can have a tour."

"Me call him?" I asked. "Why don't you call him?"

"Oh, you only want to be the leader when it comes to the decisions. You don't want to do the work like figure out the duty schedules or arrange field trips," he said scornfully.

"Hey, you're the one who wants to do everything and gets mad if I try to help. So you just go ahead and do it all by yourself. You don't need any of us!" I jumped to my feet angrily. "You can have the club all to yourself and call it Defender of the Universe!" I hated him.

Chris jumped up too, his face red and twisted.

"We didn't have these problems before you came! Everything was peaceful!"

"I'm sure it was! Maybe they just didn't know they could do better for a leader than you!"

"This has got to stop."

Chris and I tore our eyes from each other and stared at Kyle.

"You two are going to rip this group apart. We only need one leader, not fighting about anything."

"So what do you suggest, Mr. Peace-keeper?" I asked sarcastically.

Kyle's eyes went cold. "You know what your problem is, Rachel? You think if an idea isn't yours then it's not good. We all have good ideas."

Chris turned a triumphant look on me.

"And you, Chris, even if she has a good idea, you go against it just because it's hers."

It was my turn to look smug.

"I think we should close this meeting and go home and think about what we can do." U.N. pulled his stocking cap on and walked down the path without looking back. Without a word the others followed. Chris and I stood there, not looking at each other. Finally he turned and left.

I stood all by myself.

"It's all right, Rachel."

I sniffed loudly and dried my face off.

"No, it's not, Justin. I'm bossy and pushy and I'm not going to have any friends left." I pulled an ancient, ratty Kleenex from my jacket pocket and blew my nose.

"I'm your friend, Rachel."

I was busy feeling sorry for myself and I thought meanly, Oh, whoopie, a five-year-old friend.

Justin turned hurt eyes on me.

"Oh gosh, I forgot that you pick up things!"
I hugged him tightly. "I'm sorry, Justin.
You're right, age doesn't matter. You're one of
my best friends."

We sat there silently for a few minutes.

"Rachel?"

"What?"

"Did you think about my problem?"

"Yeah, Justin, I did. I was going to come
here today and tell you all this wise stuff to
help you and pretend that it was all my idea,
but I'm going to tell you the truth instead."
So I told him about my dad knowing all about
the Defenders and what he thought.

Justin didn't get upset.

"Do you think your dad is right, about me
being special in a good way?"

"Oh, I do, Justin." I leaned forward earnestly. "You know, I think you handle it very
well."

He considered that. "What did he say about
the danger coming?"

"Well, it was his idea that we check out the

police station," I admitted.

"You don't think it's bad to be a mutant?"

I exhaled noisily. "I guess everybody has their problems, Justin. I think you shouldn't worry about being a mutant. Look at us. We all know you're different and we still like you."

That brightened him up a little.

"So maybe you can help me solve my problem," I said, half joking.

He bit his bottom lip thoughtfully. "I'll tell you tomorrow."

I smiled at him and we headed home. I had to check my house for villains or evil space aliens before I unstacked the Danger Rocks.

Justin did have an idea for me the next day.

"Why don't you do something that Chris wants you to do?"

"What? I'm not doing anything for that jerk."

Justin frowned in disapproval. "Rachel, I'm trying to help you," he said firmly.

"Yeah, I know. Do you think it would do any good?"

"Yes."

"Well, what should I do?"

He even had that part thought out. "Call the police station and see if we can visit."

"Are you playing games, Justin? Sounds like you talked this over with Chris."

"It's my idea!" he flared.

"Okay, okay. Sorry."

"Are you going to do it?" he pushed.

"All right! Let's go find a phone booth." I glowered at him, but he smiled.

★ 10 ★
The Chase

Lieutenant Stefano shook each of our hands.

"So what will it be, the grand tour? Do you want to see Detention too?"

"Yes, sir," Chris answered. "But we're missing one person."

Looking around us, the Lieutenant asked, "Does she have a blue backpack?"

Packy was so excited that she crashed into Justin.

"You guys!" she gasped, breathless.

"Packy, you're late." Chris sounded annoyed.

Packy grabbed the front of Chris's jacket.

"Chris, I saw him! The man who ran over the lady!"

The Lieutenant was suddenly in front of Packy.

"Are you talking about the hit-and-run suspect, young lady?"

"Yes, sir!"

"Where and how long ago?" demanded the Lieutenant.

"He's on Dock Street, in front of that restaurant with the red sign." Packy turned to us and added, "He was with the Evil Brain!"

"I knew it!" I hissed. "We should have thought of that ourselves."

The Lieutenant was already on the phone.

"I want all available units at Dock and Main. We have the 20002 suspect in front of Waynes'. Has the Edward team hit the streets yet?" He said to Packy, "Can you tell me what he's wearing?"

Like the rest of us, Packy took her patrol seriously. She quickly handed the Lieutenant

79

a piece of paper with the information he
needed. He raised his eyebrows but took the
paper and read it off to the dispatcher. I caught
Chris's eye and grinned. Obviously the Lieutenant didn't know he was dealing with profes-
sionals. Chris grinned back.

Kyle leaned toward us to whisper, "Maybe

we should get out of the way. They'll forget about us and we can still hang around and watch."

This sounded pretty reasonable, so we quietly edged out of the Lieutenant's office and checked around for an inconspicuous place where we could watch.

"Over here!" Minh waved us into a room lined with tables set into the walls. Pencils and pens littered the tables, and books sat open.

"This must be where they write police reports," Kyle said knowledgeably.

We sat in a corner where we would be overlooked but still be close enough to the glass wall to see the comings and goings and keep an eye on the Lieutenant's office.

The Lieutenant hurried to the exit to the police parking lot. In a few seconds other officers followed him, checking their gear and buckling on gun belts.

"And just what are you kids doing in here?" A dark-haired woman stood in the doorway.

We looked at one another, disappointed to

have been discovered so soon. Finally Chris said, "We're waiting for the Lieutenant."

"Did he tell you to wait in here?"

"Well, not exactly — " Chris was interrupted by the lady's radio.

"Adam six, suspect on foot walking south on Main — "

"Edward two, Adam six, roger. Have him in sight — "

"This is Edward four, I'm going around the back."

"Adam six, Edward two, he sees us!"

"Suspect running back toward the dock."

We were all frozen, imagining what was happening downtown. The lady leaned toward the door, ready to run to her car if more help was needed.

"Adam six, this is Edward two and four. We have the suspect, repeating, we have the suspect in custody. Requesting a pickup at Dock and Mission."

We all breathed out and relaxed a little and the lady turned her attention back to us.

"Ma'am, if that's the guy that did the hit-and-run, then the Lieutenant is going to need us because we were witnesses." I shot a look of surprise at Packy. Good idea! She kept a straight face, but her eyes twinkled with pride.

The lady studied us for a few seconds.

"All right, but I want you to stay right here and don't leave this room. Got it?"

We said that we understood.

When the Lieutenant returned, he nodded approvingly at us sitting quietly in the report-writing room. I was getting warm, with my costume on underneath my clothes, but I didn't fidget. I was a Defender and I did what I had to do.

Then we went back to the Lieutenant's office and watched on a small TV screen as the officers positioned the prisoner in front of the camera. It gave me a jolt to see that face again.

Chris said, "Is that him?"

"Yes."

Chris turned back to the Lieutenant and we stood silently.

The Lieutenant gazed at us thoughtfully for a few seconds, then he said, "Thank you for your assistance. I hope you don't mind if we have the tour another time."

"No problem, Lieutenant," Chris answered gravely.

We filed out — except for Justin.

I was worried about what Justin would tell the Lieutenant. It's one thing if your own parent knows your secret identity, but you can't tell every outsider you happen to like. I waited by the door and listened.

I couldn't tell what they were saying.

Then their voices got louder as they walked toward the door. The Lieutenant crouched down so that he was at about eye level with Justin and said, "You're not talking about *evil* mutants, are you?"

Justin shook his head.

"Then I would say that mutants can count on us to protect them too."

Justin sighed, like a great load was taken off him. They both saw me standing there and

Justin reached his hand out to take mine. I held it without taking my eyes off the Lieutenant.

I didn't know what else to do, so we turned and walked down the hall. When I turned back to look, the Lieutenant was still watching us.

★ 11 ★
The Wrong Sign

In school on Thursday, I reached into my jacket pocket for something and instead found the silver star.

Something was up. Great! I hoped it wasn't Chris just wanting to tell us something like what a good job we were doing, remembering to unstack the Danger Rocks.

I went right home after school to do my chores so I could go to the meeting after dinner.

"Hey, wait for us!" I stopped and waited for Minh and Packy to catch up with me. Minh had Captain Kirk, of course. Since it was still cold, he was riding in his carrying box.

"So what's up?" I asked them. "This better be important because I can't stay out too long on a week night."

Minh shrugged.

Packy said, "Who called the meeting?"

"Heck if I know. There's Kyle. Maybe he knows."

Kyle was standing like a statue in the middle of the sidewalk, and something about that made me uneasy. When he didn't move aside but put his fingers to his lips, we stopped, confused.

"What's the matter?"

"Shhhhhhh!" He stepped lightly toward Chris and Justin's house and then waited.

I was looking around, puzzled, when Packy whispered, "The Danger Rocks!"

The three rocks were stacked against one of the two trees in the front yard.

"Oh, for — you'd think that one of those

pinheads could remember to unstack — "

"Rachel!" Kyle interrupted. "When's the last time you remember anybody forgetting to change the danger signal?"

"Well, never."

"Then what are you doing? This could be serious!"

"Okay, okay, you're right. We better act like it's real just in case. Packy, you and Kyle go around that side of that house and Minh and I will go this way. Don't let anybody see you. Report back in" — I looked at my watch — "five minutes."

"Got it!" They hunched over and ran silently across the lawn and around the garage. I waved to Minh and we went the other way. We stepped over the low fence, and I was thinking that it was a good thing they didn't have a dog as I tiptoed around the plants to get to a back window.

The window was dark.

Well, so what? So they weren't in their room. Maybe they were watching TV. I started to get a tiny bit uneasy anyway.

Minh and I slid around the corner to the back of the house, where the dining room was. The room was brightly lit. Carefully I eased my head up and peeked in the corner of the window. What I saw shocked me so much that I dropped to a crouch and covered my mouth with both hands. Minh grabbed my arm, jerked me up, and pulled me around the house. Back in the shadow of the trees, Kyle and Packy waited.

"You saw?" I squeaked. But I knew from their faces that they had.

"What?" Minh shook my sleeve.

I almost choked trying to take a breath.

"There's a guy in there and he has a gun and it's pointed at Chris and Justin's mom! What are we going to do?"

We just stared at one another with our mouths hanging open.

I started babbling, then took a couple of breaths.

"Okay, okay, let's be calm. We need to do

something. We need a plan. Okay." I thought hard for a few seconds.

"We need to tell the police. Wait!" I grabbed Kyle's sleeve as he started to get up. "Let's think this out before we get crazy." Kyle froze and then hunched down again.

"We need to give the police as much information as we can, but we have to be careful." I thought again, rapidly discarding ideas that were too dangerous or dumb.

"Okay, how about this? Kyle will go for the police. But Kyle, go to the station and see the Lieutenant. He knows we wouldn't make this up. While you're gone, we'll get as much information as we can. If we aren't here when you get back with the police, look under the first Danger Rock. We'll leave notes of anything we found out. Got it?"

"Got it!" He melted into the darkness, and we could hear the faint noises of his bike tires going off the curb.

"What should I do, Rachel?"

"Let's see, we didn't have a patrol today because of the meeting," I muttered. "Packy, didn't you do a patrol yesterday?"

"Yes."

"Good. I want you to check out the cars on this street and write down the license numbers of the ones you don't think belong here. This guy must have brought a car, but maybe he didn't park it real close to the house. Put your notes under the Danger Rock."

"What about us?" Minh watched me.

I took another deep breath.

"You and I have to find out what's going on in there and somehow let Chris and Justin know that help is coming."

"I know how we can let them know."

"How?"

"We could stick one of our star stickers on the window."

"Hey sure! Wait, I don't have them with me." What a jerk I was!

"Then we'll have to use our secret weapon."

I stared at her. "We have a secret weapon?"

She walked over to some bushes and pulled out the box.

"Captain Kirk? What can he do?"

"All we have to do is get him into the window. Justin or Chris will see him and know that we're here."

"But Minh, what if the gunman sees him? He might shoot him or something." I couldn't believe it, I was actually getting fond of that bug.

"Rachel, he won't fire that gun at a spider. Someone would hear it. I'll tell him not to run around too much," she added, meaning the spider.

She would tell him not to run around too much. Oh, great! But what else did we have? The only other person with star stickers was Justin and we sure weren't going into that house.

We heard the faint sounds of Packy returning.

"Rachel, I put Chris's mom's license number on the paper too in case the man makes them take that car."

"Good idea," I whispered. "Now wait over there by those bushes and watch for the police."

"Wait, Rachel, I have an idea."

"What?"

"Did you know that Chris and Justin's mom works in a bank?"

"She does?"

"Yeah, at the one across the street from the sandwich place. Maybe I should go down there and keep watch."

Minh nodded silently and I said, "Do it, Packy."

She sped off and I suddenly realized that I hadn't thought of a way to communicate with her. Wasn't there a pay phone on that corner? Would Packy know to answer it?

"Come on." Minh tugged me. Things were starting to move too fast.

We made our way back to the dining room window and waited. I studied the window and noted with dismay that it had a screen. I pointed to it. Minh slid a nail under the screen and tugged gently. It moved slightly.

"Unlocked," she whispered so low that I had to read her lips.

I motioned for her to hold the screen out so that I could slide the window open and push the spider through. I reached up and was just about to try the window when I heard Minh gasp and throw herself backward into the dirt. The screen slipped out of its holders and dropped off the window. I watched in horror as it fell and squished my eyes shut, waiting for the crash.

It didn't come.

I opened my eyes and saw why. By throwing herself under the window, Minh was able to catch the screen. She lay there on her back, holding the screen on her stomach. Her eyes were bugged out.

With shaking hands, I slid the window open three inches and waited for Captain Kirk to go through. Making sure his legs were clear, I slid it closed, but I heard enough of the talking inside to know that Packy had been right. The man wanted to go to the bank.

Moving in slow motion, Minh and I put the screen in some bushes. Then I slid my head up for a look. The man had his back to me, so he didn't see Captain Kirk walk slowly across the windowsill.

But Justin did.

His tear-stained eyes blinked.

The spider came to the end of the ledge and squatted down, almost invisible, unsure of what to do. I sighed with relief.

"He's never been to this house before, he's nervous," Minh whispered. "Also, he senses danger, he won't move."

Then I remembered. I grabbed the front of Minh's shirt.

"They *are* going to the bank. One of us should warn Packy." Now what, now what? You wanted to be the leader, a part of me sneered.

"I'll go," Minh was whispering. "I live closer than you, so I can get my bike quicker."

"Minh." She stopped and looked at me curiously.

"Minh, please be careful," I begged her.

She patted my arm reassuringly and was gone.

★ 12 ★

Decisions

I made my way back to the front of the house and crouched down in the shadows. My stomach was jumping around and my ears were ringing.

I didn't have long to wait.

The front door opened slowly and the man looked out. Then he pushed Chris's mom out. She turned, but he was right behind her with Justin and Chris. Justin searched the yard for us, but I didn't dare let him see me. They all got into a blue car parked behind a hedge.

Had Packy seen that car?

I watched them drive away and shivered alone in the dark.

When Kyle tapped me on the shoulder, I almost screamed.

"Come on," he whispered, pulling me back to the street. I hadn't even heard them, but there were police cars all over the street. We ran to the Lieutenant's car.

"They left," I told him.

Kyle handed him Packy's list of license plate numbers and I told him the color of the car.

"I want all of these plates run," he told an officer who had joined us.

"You don't happen to know where they are going, do you?"

"They're going to the bank! Their mom works there!"

The Lieutenant started his car and pulled away.

I stood there stunned for a few seconds, then started to run after him like a dork.

"Wait! You don't know which bank!"

Kyle caught up with me and grabbed my arm.

"He knows which bank, Rachel. On the

way over here he had the dispatcher call the records department and look up their mom's name because he said it sounded familiar. The records people found a police report with her name on it because there was trouble at the bank once and she called the police for help. The Lieutenant figured it out pretty fast."

I felt a grudging respect for the Lieutenant.

The Lieutenant must have thought of something else, because his car backed up and he leaned out of the window.

"You kids get on home now. We'll take it from here. It's not a game anymore, and I'm sure your parents are wondering where you are." He drove off.

I slapped my hand to my face.

"Oh no! I forgot! Look at the time! My parents are going to kill me!"

Kyle was watching something behind me. He said, "Uh-oh."

I glanced back and saw my mom's car. She stopped next to us and man, was she mad.

"Get in the car, Rachel," she said in that

dead calm voice that she has when she is so angry you can almost see smoke coming out of her ears. My legs went rubbery, but I managed to walk around the car and get in the passenger side. I was in mucho trouble now.

"Your father is looking for you, Kyle, and he is even angrier than I am." My mom rolled up the window and pulled away from the curb.

She didn't say anything the whole ride home.

My father was waiting on the front porch. He hustled us into the house.

"Anything new?" my mom asked him.

He shook his head grimly. Mom walked over to the police scanner and turned it up.

"All vehicles are in position, Adam six. Advise."

"All units, keep out of sight and stand by. Suspect has three hostages."

It was the Lieutenant's voice.

I had forgotten that my dad sometimes listened to his police scanner. No wonder my

102

parents were all worked up. They didn't know for sure what was going on, just that the police had a hot call. They probably figured that somebody was going around the streets shooting kids or something. You know how parents are.

I slipped off to my bedroom and sat on the edge of the bed. They were all out there. Packy and Minh were hiding at the bank somewhere, and some creep had a gun on Chris and Justin. And I was just supposed to go to bed!

"Aren't you forgetting something, Rachel?"

My mom had cooled down a little now that I was safe at home.

"I'm going, Mom." I gathered my nightshirt and robe and headed for the bathroom. I was so nervous that I dropped my robe twice.

"No reading after your bath tonight, Rachel. It's late, and I want you in bed, asleep, in twenty minutes."

I just nodded as I walked past her into the bathroom.

I turned on the water and put some pink

bubble bath in while I thought about as hard as I ever had in my whole life. When I turned off the water, I had made my decision.

I was Sketcher, temporary leader of the Defenders of the Universe, and there was evil in my town.

When I got into bed, I made myself lie still, even though I was just about turning inside out. Finally my mom came in and turned off the light.

"Good night, Rachel."

"Good night, Mom." I tried to sound sleepy.

I waited for five minutes, then I was out of there.

★ 13 ★
Crisis

I dropped to the ground outside my bedroom window. It would make too much noise if I tried to get my bike out of the garage in the dark. I would have to run. I tore out around the corner and shrieked when something crashed into me.

"It's me, Rachel," Kyle whispered frantically, taking his hand from my mouth. Then he sniffed and grinned at me.

"They made you take a bath too, huh?"

"Never mind that, come on!" I grabbed his arm and ran.

"Rachel, wait! I have my bike in the bushes!"

"Oh man, that's great!" I jumped on his bike and he climbed onto the handlebars and we took off like the wind.

It felt weird being out this late on our own. It made you want to do things that you couldn't do in the day, like lie in the street or dance on the front lawn. I pedaled until the muscles in my legs gave out, then Kyle and I traded places. We didn't talk much. Both of us were too afraid to say what we were thinking, that by the time we got there it would be over. I was very worried about something else too. If Packy or Minh got hurt or killed, it would be my fault.

Kyle hit his brakes and made a sudden left turn. We were in a narrow alley half a block from the bank. We took off our clothes and draped them over the handlebars because, of course, we had our costumes on underneath.

"Masks?" Kyle asked.

"Masks." I slipped mine over my face.

"Hold it right there."

Kyle and I froze and put our hands in the air. This was it, we were going to die. Fog appeared in front of my eyes and I knew I was going to faint. Newspaper headlines danced in my head. One said, 'Kids killed by bank robber'; the other one said, 'Hail of bullets nails local Super Heroes.' I kind of liked that last one.

"Turn around," the man's voice demanded as the flashlight outlined us on the dirty alley wall. We stared into the light.

"Lieutenant! Here's two more of them!"

Kyle and I fell against each other with relief.

"You just couldn't resist, could you?" The Lieutenant sounded angry and resigned. "Who are you two supposed to be?"

"Sketcher," I said, standing up straight.

"U.N.," Kyle said.

The Lieutenant nodded. "Well, I have Animal Princess sitting in my patrol car."

Kyle and I exchanged looks.

The Lieutenant, watching us, said sharply,

"You mean there are more of you running around?"

We nodded.

"Look, I don't think you understand. We have a very dangerous situation here. There's a guy with a gun in there. He could shoot them before he leaves the bank. If we go in there, they could get hit in the crossfire. And now I have you kids running around in masks, for God's sake."

"We're not kids, we're the Defenders of the Universe and we weren't going to get in the way. Those hostages are friends of ours!" I clamped my mouth shut, appalled that I had talked that way to an adult. I was in for it now.

The Lieutenant stared at us, then slowly shook his head.

"Put them in with the other Defender, Sergeant. And if you two get out of that car I'll have you in juvenile detention. Got that?"

When the officer opened the car door, we

slid in next to Minh. She had her mask on too. When the door closed again, she looked around us.

"Isn't Packy with you?"

"No. Don't you know where she is?" My voice squeaked.

"I couldn't find her. I searched in all our places. Where do you think she is?"

"I don't know," I groaned.

Where could Packy have gone?

★ 14 ★

Defenders of the Universe

"Maybe she got in an accident on her way here?" Kyle offered.

"Oh great." I could picture Packy's mangled body lying in the gutter on a dark street.

"Something's happening." Minh rolled the window down.

We strained to hear what was going on while the officers crouched in the dark, tensed, facing the side door of the bank. The door was slowly opening and a small head peeked out.

"Oh no! Oh no! It's Packy! They'll shoot her!" Kyle slapped his hand over my mouth and we watched, horrified, as Packy ran into the street with her hands up. The Lieutenant

dashed out, scooped her up, and sprinted behind a patrol car. Packy was hysterical, and
even at a distance we could hear her.

"He's going to shoot them! He can't get the
vault door open and he's mad and he's going
to shoot them! Hurry, hurry!"

The Lieutenant said something into the radio and the officers ran to the bank. One of
them went in the door that Packy had left
wedged open with her mask. The others ran
to the front doors, and we heard glass shatter.

We waited, holding our breath, for gun-
shots. There were none.

Then the front doors opened and the officers
were leading a man out in handcuffs. The
Lieutenant fetched Packy and walked her over
to the car we were in.

"In the car, you."

Packy climbed in next to Minh and with a
great sigh leaned her head on Minh's shoulder.

We waited silently while the Lieutenant
gave everybody orders, talked to Chris's mom,
and answered the radio. The bank manager

came and examined the bank doors, and people stood in groups, talking. We heard Chris's mom say to the Lieutenant, "I don't know how you knew what was going on and when to break in, but you saved our lives."

"We had some help," the Lieutenant said dryly.

Packy was sound asleep when the Lieutenant finally finished and came back to the car. He got in the front seat and turned to face us.

"I've got a deal to make with you kids."

Packy blinked sleepily and we waited.

"I have already had the station phone your parents" — he nodded to Packy and Minh — "to tell them that you were witnesses and were inadvertently caught up in this whole thing but that everything is fine and I'm bringing you home. As for you two" — he faced Kyle and me — "I imagine that you slipped out through back windows. So I'll drop you off near your houses so you can get back in that way. First everybody will retrieve their clothes and look normal again." He watched us and we waited for the rest of it.

"I will do this and protect your secret identities if you all swear on your honor as Defenders not to ever do anything like this again and to be in my office after school tomorrow for debriefing."

I sighed with relief. I would do anything he asked if I could go back home and get in bed. As for the rest, nothing on this entire planet could get me to do something like this again.

"Do we have a deal?"

We didn't even have to look at one another. We all said, "Yes, sir."

"Okay, let's get going." He turned back around and started the car.

★ 15 ★
Debriefing

We were sitting in the Lieutenant's office and Packy was telling her story.

"... and when they went into the bank, the piece of curtain that covers the door blew out and got caught in the door so it didn't close all the way. I went in real quiet on my hands and knees and crawled under the desks until I turned the corner and was in the back part of the bank. Then I just waited."

"What exactly did you think you were going to do then?" the Lieutenant asked, curious.

"I didn't know," Packy admitted.

"How come the bank robber couldn't get the vault open?" I wanted to know. "Couldn't your mom just use the combination and get it open?"

Chris shook his head. "You can't just open a bank vault any time you want. They're on timers, so when the bank closes for the day, Mom or the manager sets the timer to open the vault at the right time the next morning. Mom couldn't have opened the vault even if he shot Justin and me."

I shivered. "How did that guy get into your house?"

"We were eating dinner and the doorbell rang and Justin answered it. We thought it was you guys. The guy shoved Justin down and walked right in."

"Wait a minute," Kyle interrupted. "If you guys were eating dinner, that meant you had been home for a while. How come you didn't move the Danger Rocks?"

Chris frowned. "I did move them."

We all looked at Justin. He said shyly, "I put them back because the danger was close."

"Oh, Justin." I put my arms around him.

The Lieutenant's phone buzzed.

"I'll be right there." He told us, "Stay here until I get back."

"Chris, did you know we were outside the house?" Minh asked.

Chris smiled. "Not until I saw the screen drop off the window and Captain Kirk put in." He studied all of us a minute. "I want you guys to know that I'm proud of you." He faced me. "Rachel is a good leader. I hope we can come up with something so we don't fight anymore."

"I have come up with something!" Kyle grinned at us. "That's why I called the meeting for last night. How about this? Chris is the leader, but Rachel is the adviser. When Chris makes a decision he can have Rachel advise him, but he has the final word. And Rachel can call us all together if she doesn't like one of Chris's decisions."

Justin giggled. We knew what TV show had inspired Kyle.

"What do you think?"

I considered it. "Sounds good to me."

The Lieutenant returned and sat down at his desk.

"I have one suggestion for you kids and one request."

We eyed him warily.

"First of all, if you have any more suspicious observations, I want you to write them up as a report and give them to me. You can mail them to the station here, directed to me so that no one else will read them. Oh, and leave the Evil Brain, as you call him, alone. He is a respected member of this community. He was only giving directions to the hit-and-run suspect."

I watched my toes, embarrassed.

"Second, I would like something from you."

Uh-oh, I thought, suddenly afraid. He's going to ask us for our costumes so we won't get into any more trouble.

"I would like a picture of you for my desk — in full costume with masks."

We stared at him with our mouths open.

Packy squealed with excitement. "Oh, let's do it, Chris!"

Chris started to say something but stopped suddenly and turned to me.

"What do you think, Rachel?"

"I think we should do it. After all, Batman used to help Commissioner Gordon."

Everybody cheered.

So that's how I got to be a Defender and why I'm supposed to be typing up the Lieutenant's weekly report on our patrols instead of writing this. Everything worked out pretty well. Our picture looks great on the Lieutenant's desk, and no matter who asks him, he always says that we are a closely guarded secret.

There's only one thing.

Justin says that a UFO is approaching Earth, but he's not sure where it's going to land. Chris says Justin has seen *Close Encounters* too many times, but I keep remembering those

Danger Rocks, so, just in case, I check the sky
every night before I go to bed.

You never know.